SOCCER AROUND THE WORLD

By Tracey West

Illustrated by Jeff Albrecht Studios

ISBN 0-439-75375-
All Major League Soccer properties are used by permission a...
Nike and the Swoosh (design) are registered trademarks ...
Copyright © 2005 Scholastic Entertainment I...
SCHOLASTIC, MAYA & MIGUEL and logos are tr...
12 11 10 9 8 7 6 5 4 3 2 1   5 6
Printed in the U.S.A.
First printing, September 2005

SCHOLASTIC INC.

New York   Toronto   London   Auckland   Sydney
Mexico City   New Delhi   Hong Kong   Buenos Aires

MVFOL

One afternoon, Maya hurried home from soccer practice. She dribbled her soccer ball as she ran.

Near the Santos family's apartment, an athletic young man surprised Maya. He stole the ball away from her, then bounced it off of his head!

"Hey!" Maya shouted.

Maya's father laughed. "This is
my new friend, Eddie Johnson,"
said Mr. Santos. "I met him
when he was shopping at
our pet store. Eddie plays
on the Major League
Soccer team FC Dallas."

"Sorry I stole your ball," Eddie told Maya. "When I see a soccer ball, I can't help myself."

"Wow!" Maya said. "A real live soccer star!"

"Eddie's coming over to our apartment to meet the family," said Mr. Santos.

"Eddie is staying for dinner," Abuela said.
Maya smiled. "That's good news!"

Then Miguel rushed in, waving a piece of paper. "I have bad news!" he announced. "They might cut the school soccer program! The school board is voting on the cut at the end of the week."

Mrs. Santos read the paper and frowned. "It's true," she said. "The board says they're having budget problems. Next year, there may not be any more school soccer!"

Then Miguel noticed Eddie. His eyes bugged out of his head. "Eddie Johnson!" he exclaimed. "What are you doing in our apartment?"

"Right now, I'm being sad for your school," Eddie replied. To cheer everyone up, Eddie told stories about playing soccer around the world with the United States National Team.

Maya jumped up, her ponytail holder flashing brightly. "*¡Eso es!*" she shouted. "*¡Tengo una idea!*"

Mr. Santos smiled. "Maya scores more ideas than you score goals, Eddie," he said.

Maya quickly described her plan.

"I like it!" Miguel said. "But I think we will need some help."

The next day, Maya and Miguel got all of their friends together to meet Eddie. They explained Maya's plan.

"I call it Plan SOS," Maya said. "Save Our Soccer!"

Finally, it was time for the school board meeting. The treasurer explained the problem — there wasn't enough money in the budget to afford the soccer team. It would have to be cut.

"Does anyone have anything to say?" asked the president.

"We do!" said Maya and Miguel at the same time. They jumped onstage.

"This is a little show we call 'Soccer Around the World'!" Maya said.

All the kids joined Maya and Miguel onstage. "Soccer is one of the most popular sports in the world," Miguel began.

"Many countries have a national team," Maya continued. "They play in a contest called the World Cup every four years. It is the biggest soccer game on Earth!"

Theo stepped up. "Soccer began in England in the middle of the 1800s," he said.

"It is called football there. The game became so popular in England that it soon spread all over the world."

Chrissy stepped up next. "Brazil has the greatest national soccer team in the world," she said. "They have won the World Cup five times."

"That is more than any other country!" Chrissy continued. "One of the best players ever comes from Brazil. His name is Pelé. In the 1970s, he played here in the United States!"

Next it was Andy's turn. "Soccer is usually played outside," he said, "so it took awhile to get popular in colder countries like Denmark and Sweden."

"But now they both have strong national teams," Andy added. "They even started a winter league to stay in shape during the cold months."

GREAT MOMENT: DENMARK WON THE EUROPEAN CHAMPIONSHIP IN 1992

SWEDEN'S NATIONAL LANGUAGE: SWEDISH

DENMARK'S NATIONAL LANGUAGE: DANISH

FUN FACT: DENMARK'S FANS ARE CALLED "ROLIGANS." THEY HAVE LOTS OF SPIRIT!

Maggie came up next. "It took a long time for soccer to catch on in Japan," she said. "Then, in 1981, a comic book about soccer came out. It got people interested in the sport."

"Now the national team is more popular than ever," said Maggie. "Some fans go to games dressed like characters from *anime*. *Anime* is the Japanese word for cartoons!"

TOP NATIONAL LEAGUE: JAPAN PROFESSIONAL FOOTBALL LEAGUE

JAPAN'S NATIONAL LANGUAGE: JAPANESE

GREAT MOMENT: WON BRONZE MEDAL IN 1968 OLYMPICS

GREAT MOMENT: PLAYED IN THE 2002 WORLD CUP

Next, Tito ran up. "Second to Brazil, Italy has one of the best teams in the world," he said.

"They have won the World Cup three times!" Tito exclaimed. "The national team wears blue jerseys. That is how they got their nickname — the Blue Squad!"

Next came Maya's turn. "In the United States, women rule the soccer field," she said. "The national women's team has won the women's World Cup twice!"

"Soccer is also very popular with American kids," added Maya. "There are more than 15 million players between the ages of 5 and 19!"

NATIONAL LANGUAGE OF U.S.: ENGLISH

BIGGEST MEN'S LEAGUE: MAJOR LEAGUE SOCCER

FAMOUS WOMEN'S SOCCER PLAYER: MIA HAMM

GREAT MOMENT: WOMEN'S SECOND WORLD CUP WIN IN 1999

"Now let's hear from a real live soccer star,"
Miguel said. "Our new friend, Eddie Johnson!"

"I have been all over the world," said Eddie. "Kids play soccer in Africa, Europe, Asia, and Latin America. They stay in shape, they learn teamwork, and they have fun. Soccer makes their lives better."

"We need soccer in our school," Maya said.
"It is a way to connect us to the rest of the
world," Miguel added.